For Freddie —T.T.

To my godmother and Aunt Alison.
Thanks for all the marshmallows. —T.B.

Text copyright © 2020 by Todd Tarpley

Jacket art and interior illustrations copyright © 2020 by Tom Booth

All rights reserved. Published in the United States by Doubleday, an imprint of Random House Children's Books, a division of Penguin Random House LLC, New York.

Doubleday and the colophon are registered trademarks of Penguin Random House LLC.

Visit us on the Web! rhcbooks.com

Educators and librarians, for a variety of teaching tools, visit us at RHTeachersLibrarians.com

Library of Congress Cataloging-in-Publication Data
Names: Tarpley, Todd, author. | Booth, Tom, illustrator.
Title: Library books are not for eating! / by Todd Tarpley ; illustrated by Tom Booth.
Description: First edition. | New York : Doubleday, [2020] |
Summary: "Ms. Bronte loves being a teacher, but she has one small problem . . . she also really loves eating books. Did I mention she's also a dinosaur?" —Provided by publisher.
Identifiers: LCCN 2017043898 | ISBN 978-1-5247-7168-3 (hc) | ISBN 978-1-5247-7169-0 (glb) | ISBN 978-1-5247-7170-6 (ebk)
Subjects: | CYAC: Stories in rhyme. | Dinosaurs—Fiction. | Teachers—Fiction. | Books and reading—Fiction. | Food habits—Fiction. | Humorous stories.
Classification: LCC PZ8.3.T1476 Li 2020 | DDC [E]—dc23

MANUFACTURED IN CHINA
10 9 8 7 6 5 4 3 2 1
First Edition

LIBRARY BOOKS
ARE NOT FOR EATING!

By Todd Tarpley

Illustrated by Tom Booth

Doubleday Books
for Young Readers

The day Ms. Bronte came to school,
story time was extra cool.
She told great jokes, was never mean.
Biggest smile you'd ever seen.

One small problem,
couldn't beat it.
Once she read a book . . .

. . . SHE'D EAT IT!

She'd say "The End," you'd hear a crunch,
then three or four more books by lunch.
"Ms. Bronte," kids would keep repeating,
"library books are **NOT** for eating!"

Ms. Bronte promised with a roar
that she'd be eating books no more.
But soon as story time was done . . .

Oops! There'd go another one.

Ms. McSmartly called her in.
"Ms. Bronte, where do I begin?
You're eating books! That isn't right.
You need to curb your appetite.
I think you know where this is leading. . . .
Library books are **NOT** for eating!"

READ MORE

Ms. Bronte promised with a roar
that she'd be eating books no more.
When Ms. McSmartly turned her head,
SHE ATE UP ALL HER BOOKS INSTEAD!

At lunchtime when she ate two more,
the lunchroom lady stomped the floor.
"Ms. Bronte, you must change your diet.
Books taste yucky. Don't deny it.

"Instead of books, try something new—
my cottage cheese and meatball stew!
We've got to rearrange your feeding.
Library books are **NOT** for eating!"

Ms. Bronte promised with a roar
that she'd be eating books no more.
She took one bite of cottage cheese . . .

. . . THEN ATE THREE BOOKS OF RECIPES!

She took a walk to clear her head.
Down to the soccer field she fled.
Coach Burly blew his whistle loudly,
pointing to his players proudly.

"I've got problems of my own:
a soccer field that's overgrown.
Can't mow the grass, can't pick the weeds.
You're not the only one with needs.
Be a winner! No more cheating. . . .
Library books are **NOT** for eating!"

Ms. Bronte promised with a roar
that she'd be eating books no more.
But as Coach Burly turned his gaze . . .
SHE ATE HIS BOOK OF SOCCER PLAYS!

Ms. Bronte packed her bags that day.
"I'm sorry, but I cannot stay.
It's not that I find books so yummy,
but nothing else here fills my tummy.
If I could find a bulb or seed,
a blade of grass, a bush, a weed . . ."

Suddenly her plan was clear:
She'd make the wild weeds disappear!
All she had to do was eat 'em—
let her appetite defeat them.

Now Ms. Bronte just eats weeds.
They fill her dietary needs.
The soccer team has gone unbeaten.
Not a single book's been eaten.

Every morning right at nine,
Ms. Bronte leads the story time.

And every afternoon at four,
she's on the sidelines keeping score.

The soccer field is good as new.

Kids run and kick where weeds once grew.

The moral of this tale you're reading . . .

Library books are **NOT** for eating!

A happy tale this might have been. . . .

But then they hired Mr. Finn. . . .